AMAZON ORIGINAL

W9-BTM-871

Tumble Leaf

The Tinsel Tree Celebration

Adapted by Lara Bergen

Text based on the episode "Tinsel Tree Topper" written by Steven Darancette.

© 2017 Amazon Content Services LLC.
Tumble Leaf © 2013-2017 Amazon Content Services LLC.

Published by Two Lions, New York

www.apub.com

Amazon, the Amazon logo, and Two Lions are trademarks of Amazon.com, Inc., or its affiliates.

ISBN-13: 9781477809037 (paperback)
ISBN-10: 1477809031 (paperback)

Book design by Tanya Ross-Hughes

Printed in China

two lions

It was a chilly day in Tumble Leaf when . . . *jingle-jangle!*, the chimes above Fig's balcony rang. That could mean only one thing! "Something new is in the Finding Place!" Fig told his best friend, Stick.

"Let's go see what it is!" said Fig.

"*Brrlllll!*" Stick agreed.

Fig and Stick hurried to the Finding Place.
"I wonder what we'll find today?" asked Fig
as he went over to the treasure chest.

"Stick, look! We found snowshoes!" Fig said. *"Brrrlll, brrrrlllll!"* Stick was excited, too.

They couldn't wait to try them out. This was a great day for snowshoes.

Fig and Stick bundled up and went onto the snowy deck.
"Sparkling snow snails, Stick!" said Fig. "It looks like the whole world
is covered in mashed potatoes. And I have the perfect *mashers*!

"With these snowshoes, we can **mash,
mash,
mash**

our way to the top of Mount Tinsel!"
He was eager to meet his friends
at the annual Tinsel Tree Celebration.

Fig picked up the very special decoration he needed for the party. "I'm going to put this tree topper on the *tippity-top* of the Tinsel Tree for all to see!"

He looked up at Mount Tinsel and saw his friends. "Come on," he said. "Everyone's waiting for us. Mount Tinsel, here we come!" "*Brrrlllllll!*" cheered Stick.

There were so many icy hills on the way to Mount Tinsel, and Fig was in a hurry! He slipped ... and slid ... and—*"Whoops!"*—fell down.

"We just have to take one

slippity

step at a time," Fig said and then ...

"Whooooaa!" Fig fell again, sliding down one

slippity-slidey

hill and up another.

Suddenly the Tinsel Tree topper went flying . . .

. . . into a big mound of
slippity snow.

"Oh, no! It's stuck," groaned Fig
as he tried to pull it free.

"Let me figure this out,"
Fig began when—

"Whoooaaaa!" He slid backward down one hill, then up another!

"*Rumble Leaf, Tumble Leaf!*

That was **queasy ski-sy!**" cried Fig.

"Brrlll! Brrlll!" Stick agreed.
He was still dizzy!

"Standing on these hills
is sure not easy!" Fig said.

But Stick had an idea. *"Brrrlll! Brrll!"*
"Good idea," Fig said. "Let's do the Caterpillar Crawl."
They crawled up a hill on their bellies.

At the top, Fig said, "Maybe I'll do the Snowshoe Shuffle."
He moved his snowshoes back and forth, sending snow and ice flying.

"Snowy snout, I figured it out!"

"Look how flat this snow hill is now! I'm going to use my snowshoes
to scrape the ice away and free the topper!" Fig announced.
Fig shuffled his way to the tree topper. Then he took off his snowshoe
and used it to **scra-a-a-pe** at the ice until . . .

. . . he pulled the topper out of the snow.
"Hooray, it's *freeee*!" Fig cheered. "And now everyone
will see it on top of the Tinsel Tree!"
"*Brrllll, brrrllll!*" Stick cheered, too.

Fig and Stick started toward
Mount Tinsel. They were so
close they could hear music
from the celebration.

Stopping for a moment to rest, Fig set
the tree topper and Stick on a log.

Suddenly the log
slid away!

"Hang on, Stick! I'm coming!" Fig yelled, running after his friend.

"Brrlllllllllll!" called Stick.

Fig slid on his belly after the log.

"Wheeeee!"

Finally he caught up, and Stick
happily hopped onto his arm.
"Brrlll, brrllll!"
Fig laughed. "You're welcome."

But the log kept on sliding and went sailing over a hill . . .
along with the tree topper!

Fig climbed to where the tree topper had disappeared.
It was nowhere to be found. "*Vanishing valley.* I lost the topper
in the snow!" Fig said. "How am I going to find it now?"

"I found the topper!" Fig exclaimed. But it was broken in two.
"Oh, no," Fig gasped. "I've ruined the Tinsel Tree Celebration for everyone!
We'd better go tell our friends."
"*Brrllll,*" Stick said sadly.

Up on Mount Tinsel, Fig's friends were busy trimming the Tinsel Tree.
Maple and Gourd were there, along with Pine and little Hedge and Zucchini
and Rutabaga and their chicks, Butternut and Squash.
"Seeing the Tinsel Tree topper at the *tippity-top* is my favorite
part of the day," Hedge said.
But where were Fig and Stick ... and the topper? The tree trimming just wasn't
the same without Fig and Stick. So the friends went to find them.

The friends walked and walked. Finally they found Fig and Stick!
"Now that we found you," said Pine, "let the Tinsel Tree Celebration begin!"
"We can't," Fig told his friends. "I broke the topper.
I'm sorry. I ruined the celebration."

"Oh, Fig," said Maple, "we don't need the Tinsel Tree topper to celebrate."
"Or even a tree," Hedge added. "All we really need is . . ."

"... me?" asked Fig as his friends gave him a big hug.

"Since this is where *you* are, this is where we'll celebrate!" Pine declared.

"Without tinsel or trimmings?" Fig asked.

"We've got plenty of snow," Maple said.

That gave Fig an idea. He used his snowshoes
to scra-a-a-pe and sculpt a snow tree.
And they found the best tree topper of all . . .

. . . Fig!

"We don't need a tree topper when we've got you, Fig!" laughed Maple.
And just like that, they had the most festive tree trimming ever.